For Mom and Dad—B.W.

Library of Congress Cataloging-in-Publication Data available.

ISBN 978-1-4521-5014-7

Manufactured in China.

MIX
Paper from
responsible sources
FSC™ C104723

Design by Jennifer Tolo Pierce.
Typeset in Adobe Garamond.
The illustrations in this book were rendered in a variety of
media, including cut paper, colored pencil, oil pastels, marker,
and the computer.

10 9 8 7 6 5 4 3 2

Chronicle Books LLC
680 Second Street
San Francisco, California 94107
www.chroniclekids.com

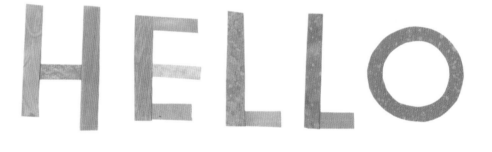

HELLO

Brendan Wenzel

chronicle books · san francisco

Hello Hello

Black and White

Hello Color

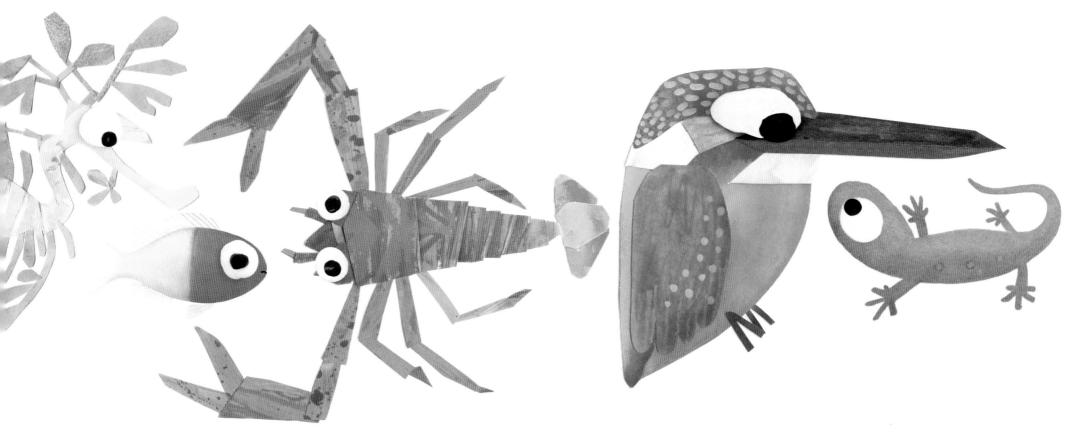

Hello Bright.

Hello Stripes

Hello Spots

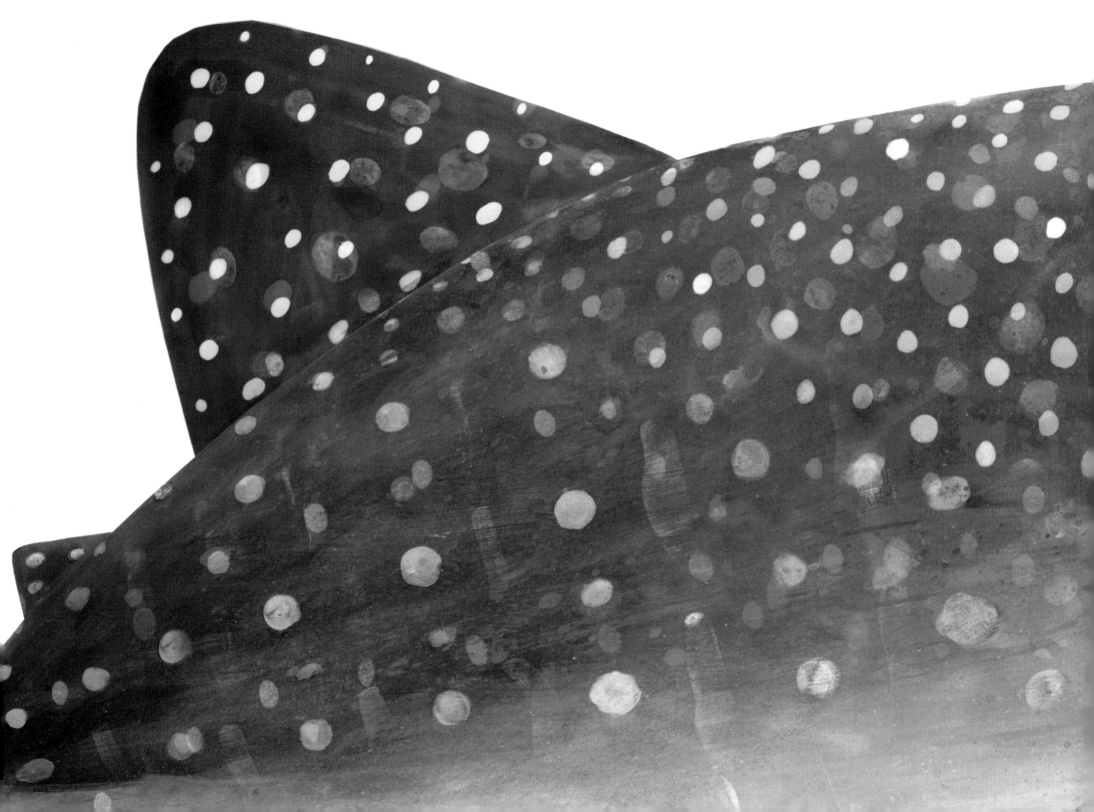

Hello Giant

Hello Not.

Hello Tongue,

Ears, Hands,

and Nose

Hello Pattern

Hello Pose.

Hello Shape

Hello Show

Hello Wonder

Hello WHOA!

Hello Quiet

Hello Loud

Hello Wild

Hello Proud.

Hello Beauty

Hello Bend

Hello Neighbor

Hello Friend.

Hello Roars,
Peeps, Chirps,
and Chants

Hello Song

and Hello Dance.

A world to see

A world to know.

Where to begin?

Hello Hello.

A Note from the Author

You have just said hello to some of my favorite animals. Their colors, shapes, sounds, patterns, habits, and strange hairdos make the world a more vibrant and fascinating place. Each one is a vital part of the ecosystem it inhabits.

Sadly, many of these creatures are in trouble—considered to be Near Threatened, Vulnerable, Endangered, or Critically Endangered by the International Union for Conservation of Nature. A species can become threatened for many reasons, like habitat loss, poaching, or climate change.

Many people don't know a lot of these animals even exist. You can help change that! Find out more about them. Head to the library, go on the internet, and share your interest and enthusiasm with everyone you know. You could even write a letter to one of the incredible conservationists working to protect them and keep the places they live safe. The more that people know about these creatures, the better the chance they will share this planet with us for many years to come.

It starts with saying hello.

Animals *In order of appearance*

1. house cat	**8.** king parrot	**15.** tiger—*Endangered*
2. American black bear	**9.** leafy sea dragon—*Near Threatened*	**16.** cheetah—*Vulnerable*
3. giant panda—*Vulnerable*	**10.** bicolor dottyback	**17.** yellow boxfish
4. plains zebra—*Near Threatened*	**11.** squat lobster	**18.** whale shark—*Endangered*
5. three-stripe damselfish	**12.** common kingfisher	**19.** veiled chameleon
6. blue damselfish	**13.** eastern newt	**20.** aardvark
7. rainbow agama	**14.** tiger salamander	**21.** Senegal galago

Source for conservation status: The International Union for Conservation of Nature at iucnredlist.org

22. proboscis monkey—*Endangered*

23. elephant seal

24. green sea turtle—*Endangered*

25. giant armadillo—*Vulnerable*

26. Sunda pangolin—*Critically Endangered*

27. Jackson's chameleon

28. rhinoceros hornbill—*Near Threatened*

29. bare-necked umbrellabird—*Endangered*

30. dainty tree frog

31. mute swan

32. platypus—*Near Threatened*

33. North American beaver

34. Brazilian porcupine

35. Western long-beaked echidna—*Critically Endangered*

36. Northern brown kiwi—*Endangered*

37. Southern cassowary—*Vulnerable*

38. green basilisk

39. Atlantic sailfish

40. narwhal—*Near Threatened*

41. blue bird of paradise—*Vulnerable*

42. blue morpho

43. owl butterfly

44. Northern saw-whet owl

45. secretary bird—*Vulnerable*

46. lionfish

47. common cuttlefish

48. common octopus

49. common hippopotamus—*Vulnerable*

50. walrus—*Vulnerable*

51. African bush elephant—*Vulnerable*

52. African lion—*Vulnerable*

53. golden lion tamarin—*Endangered*

54. emperor tamarin

55. Inca tern—*Near Threatened*

56. crested partridge—*Near Threatened*

57. grey-crowned crane—*Endangered*

58. Sulawesi lined gliding lizard

59. greater glider—*Vulnerable*

60. Major Mitchell's cockatoo

61. superb lyrebird

62. ring-tailed lemur—*Endangered*

63. human

64. Sumatran orangutan—*Critically Endangered*

65. ribbon seal

66. mimic octopus

67. blue-ringed octopus

68. brownbanded bamboo shark—
Near Threatened

69. blue grouper

70. gang-gang cockatoo

71. red-bellied newt

72. mudpuppy

73. axolotl—*Critically Endangered*

74. American flamingo

75. red-crowned crane—
Endangered

76. Araripe manakin—
Critically Endangered

77. red tile starfish

78. Marañón poison frog—*Endangered*

79. strawberry poison dart frog

80. blue poison dart frog

81. tiger-leg monkey frog

82. golden poison frog—*Endangered*

83. yellow-winged bat

84. brown long-eared bat

85. Amazon River dolphin

86. red panda—*Endangered*

87. musk ox

88. giant anteater—*Vulnerable*

89. crested rat

90. aardwolf

91. Western blue-tongued skink

92. giraffe—*Vulnerable*